For Rita
and Brendan,
good friends

M.W.

For Paul,
Nick, and Emma,
my children

J.B.

First published 1993 by
Walker Books Ltd
87 Vauxhall Walk,
London SE11 5HJ

This edition published 1995

10 9 8 7 6 5 4 3 2

Text © 1993 Martin Waddell
Illustrations © 1993 Jill Barton

Printed in Hong Kong

This book has been
typeset in Lucida.

British Library Cataloguing
in Publication Data
A catalogue record for this book is
available from the British Library.

ISBN 0-7445-3641-3

LITTLE
MO

Written by

Martin Waddell

Illustrated by

Jill Barton

WALKER BOOKS
AND SUBSIDIARIES
LONDON • BOSTON • SYDNEY

Little Mo looked at the ice
and she liked it.

BUMP!

Little Mo got up   and tried sliding again.

BUMP!

A Big One came to help her.

More Big Ones came out on the ice,

sliding and gliding around Little Mo.

They were her friends, all of them.

It was nice on the ice and she loved it.

The Big Ones whizzed and they whirled
and they twisted and twirled and
they raced and they jumped.

BUMP!   BUMP!

BUMP! BUMP!

Little Mo started to cry and she turned away.
She didn't like the ice any more.

"It was all my idea,"
Little Mo said to herself.

The Big Ones got tired and went home.

They forgot Little Mo.

Little Mo looked at the ice
and she liked it again.

She slid and … and

and

she fell. BUMP!

She got up and then she
did it again without falling,

and again

and again

and again …

all by herself,
sliding about on the ice

and Little Mo loved it.

MORE WALKER PAPERBACKS
For You to Enjoy

Also by Martin Waddell

THE PIG IN THE POND
illustrated by Jill Barton
Highly Commended for the Kate Greenaway Medal
One hot day, an amazing event occurs on Nelligan's farm.
"Pure fun… An excellent combination of text and illustration with a satisfying finale." *The Daily Telegraph*
0-7445-3153-5 £4.99

THE HAPPY HEDGEHOG BAND
illustrated by Jill Barton
Deep in the heart of Dickon Wood,
Harry and his hedgehog band are drumming and making happy music.
"A celebration of noise, admirably conveyed in Jill Barton's illustrations,
in which young children will want to join." *The Bookseller*
0-7445-3049-0 £4.50

OWL BABIES
illustrated by Patrick Benson
On a tree in the woods, three baby owls, Sarah and Percy and Bill,
wait for their Owl Mother to come home.
"Touchingly beautiful… Drawn with exquisite delicacy…
The perfect picture book." *The Guardian*
0-7445-3167-5 £4.50

SQUEAK-A-LOT
illustrated by Virginia Miller
Shortlisted for the Mother Goose Award,
this is the exuberantly noisy tale
of a little mouse, looking for someone to play with.
"A gift for storytellers, this is ideal for letting off excess energy
at bedtime and in groups." *The Bookseller*
0-7445-3047-4 £4.99

Walker Paperbacks are available from most booksellers, or by post from B.B.C.S., P.O. Box 941, Hull, North Humberside HU1 3YQ
24 hour telephone credit card line 01482 224626

To order, send: Title, author, ISBN number and price for each book ordered, your full name and address,
cheque or postal order payable to BBCS for the total amount and allow the following for postage and packing:
UK and BFPO: £1.00 for the first book, and 50p for each additional book to a maximum of £3.50.
Overseas and Eire: £2.00 for the first book, £1.00 for the second and 50p for each additional book.

Prices and availability are subject to change without notice.